# The Heart Wants What It Wants

### DEANN SOLEIL

*To those who know what they want in their relationship...*
*just go for it.*

# Contents

# Tropes and Triggers

- Age Gap (23/45)
- Ex-Boyfriend's Father
- Secret Relationship
- Valentine's Day Romance
- Open Door Romance From Page One
- Short Story to Read in One Sitting

# *Blurb:*

After a year of being with the man she cares deeply for, Natalya must make one big decision. Does she continue to stay hidden or move on to better things?

Brandon, who's no other than her ex-boyfriend's father, wants to show her the world but fears what the public might say.

With Valentine's Day just a few days away, they must decide: will they part ways forever or let love win?

# Playlist

The Heart Wants What It Wants - Selena Gomez
All of Me - John Legend
Love Me Like You Do - Ellie Goulding
Love on the Brain - Rihanna
Tennessee Whiskey - Chris Stapleton
Dilemma - Nelly (Feat. Kelly Rowland)
We Belong Together - Mariah Carey

## CHAPTER 1

# Natalya

"Fuck me harder, daddy," I call out. The way Brandon fucks me has me begging for more each time.

"I love the way your pussy grips my dick, Nat," he says as he begins to pick up his pace.

He has me bent over on my knees, and he's hitting spots that I never thought would be hit before. He might not be massive, but he's pierced and knows what he is doing.

Brandon reaches around to the front of my body and grips my neck, applying just enough pressure to start to bring my body over the edge.

"Brandon," I moan out as I can feel my pussy begin to pulsate around him. *Fuck he brings me to an orgasm so fast.*

"I'm about to cum," he says before slowing

down. I can feel him begin to twitch inside of me as he reaches his breaking point.

We sit like this for a few seconds before he pulls out of me. He slowly pulls the condom off as he walks to the bathroom, to grab a washcloth to clean me up with.

"You felt so good like you always do," he says as he slowly wipes the washcloth along my pussy.

"You know that you don't have to butter me up after we fuck, right?" I say as I roll my eyes.

"Don't be like that. You know I like being with you and being inside of you."

"I do, but when can this not be a secret anymore? I'm getting tired of us fucking behind closed doors and not being able to show others what we have."

"Natalya, you know this thing that we have between us is complicated. Being your ex-boyfriend's father doesn't make this easy. Imagine how others would feel if they saw us together," he says while rubbing his fingers across my face.

"Whatever. We broke up for a reason so why the fuck does his opinion matter? Oh wait, it doesn't. If you want to be a little pussball and not show the world who I am to you, then why are we doing this? It's been a year of this, and I don't think I can do this anymore."

I can feel the tears start to well up in my eyes. I don't want this to be the end of something good, but I can't be kept hidden anymore. With Valentine's

Day a couple days away, I hate seeing all the couples together knowing that I'm being hidden from the one person that I have spent so much time with.

"Natalya, I don't want to disappoint you, but I really don't know what we can do about this relationship. Give me some time to think about everything and if it's the right decision to go public with us. I do love you."

*Fuck this isn't the way that I wanted things to go. I just wish he would just show the world how much I mean to him.*

"If you love me, then you should put some actions behind those words," I say while putting my clothes back on.

Before he can respond, I grab all of my things and make my way out of his house to my car.

## CHAPTER 2
### *Brandon*

I hate that she just walked out and didn't give me a kiss before doing so. She keeps bringing up this conversation of us needing to be public, but I haven't really entertained the idea with her.

On the back end of things, I was able to sit down with my son a few days ago and let him know the feelings that I have for Natalya, which went way better than expected.

*After a long day of work, Evan and I decided it would be best to catch up, so I invited him over for dinner. I've been harboring some feelings for his ex-girlfriend and decided after fooling around with her for a year, it was time to see if he is okay with everything going on.*

*I decided to make him some chicken, rice, and green beans for dinner before we sit down and have a serious conversation.*

*"Thanks, dad, for cooking. It's been a little bit since I*

*had one of your homemade meals. My roommates and I often
don't cook, so I'm always grateful when we can sit down and
eat together."*

*"We definitely need to do this more often. I do want to
talk to you about something if that's okay with you," I say.*

*He gives me a questioning look, wondering where this
conversation is going to go.*

*"I'm just going to rip off the Band-Aid. Natalya and I
have been seeing each other over the last year. I want to make
things public with her, but I don't want you to feel any type
of way about it. I know she was your girlfriend, but y'all
weren't together for long. Would you be fine with me telling
others about our relationship?"*

*Instead of him getting serious, he actually lets out a
laugh instead.*

*"Dad, you've done a terrible job hiding that y'all have
been together. I've seen the signs and see her name come
across your phone sometimes. If you want her, then go
for it."*

*"Well damn, that was easier than I thought it
would be."*

I'm truly glad he was on board with the two of us
being together. I thought I was being cautious with
messaging her, but I guess I wasn't.

After the conversation, I had been thinking about
different ways I can show Natalya how much I care
about her and how I want to shout to the world she's
mine. I have all these ideas, but I don't know which

one is the best. I look at my checklist to see which ideas are feasible and which aren't.

There are so many different ideas that I would love to carry out because this girl deserves the world, but with such little time until Valentine's Day it makes it hard to do. *Why didn't I start to plan this earlier?*

# CHAPTER 3
## Natalya

Part of me hates the way I ended things with Brandon earlier. I might have overreacted some, but after a year of doing whatever this is between the two of us, it's time for him to grow a pair of balls and show me he really wants me.

There's always an excuse with him as to why we can't go out in public. Shoot, we can go out and just hang out as friends. There doesn't have to be any sign of affection between us, just us hanging out, but I can't even get that.

He fucks me so good behind closed doors that he has me crawling back to him anytime I get mad at him. I need to just suck it up and realize that there isn't going to be a public us. Instead, it will always just be me or him hitting each other up to come over and have some mind-blowing sex that neither of us can resist.

I decide to try to block out my feelings of being upset with him and send him a text to meet up tonight.

> Me: Sorry about earlier. You down to meet up tonight?

> Brandon: All good. Come to my house at 5pm

> Me: See you then.

> Brandon:

I think I'm going to do something a little different tonight. I make my way to my closet and find a black silky robe and a red lingerie set to go with it. Normally when it comes to him, I don't dress up in anything like this, but I feel like this is perfect with it being the holiday season and all.

Once I pick out my outfit for the night, I decide to read and take a little nap before I need to start getting ready for the night ahead of me.

A FEW HOURS PASS AND IT'S FINALLY 4:00 IN the afternoon. I ended up sleeping a little longer than I expected to, but I still have enough time to get myself ready for the night. I head into the shower and exfoliate my whole body. The smell of vanilla on my skin is perfect.

Once I'm all finished in the shower, I decide that I want to curl my hair for the night. For once, I want to feel sexy for Brandon and show off how good I can look. Since I have one of those fancy hair machines, I can straighten and curl my hair in less than thirty minutes which makes this so efficient.

I continue to get ready and apply a light amount of makeup on my face. Once I slip into my outfit, I put on some floral perfume along my wrist, neck, and outfit.

*Damn I smell good.* I hope this has him wanting to devour me more than he already does when we're together.

I look at the time and see it is 4:45 PM. *It looks like it's time for me to go.* I grab my bag and make my way to the car. I blare some country music through my speakers as I make my way over to Brandon's house. I got lucky to find an apartment not too far from him, so it takes me no time to get to him.

The lease for my apartment is up in three months, so I hope he decides that he wants to take the next step and allow me to move in with him. If not, I think I might just move to a different area and start fresh. It's going to be hard moving on from him, but sometimes you have to leave those who you love the most.

I can't think about that though. I'm going to go into tonight with an open mind and get off for the second time today.

For Brandon being older, he surely has good stamina. He can go for hours if I would let him, but this pussy often needs a break. He's so aggressive with the way he fucks me that he brings me over the edge quicker than any man ever could before.

I've always been hesitant about any type of anal play because it seemed like it would hurt. Last month I let my guard down though and let Brandon fuck me in the ass. Boy, let me tell you, it felt so good. He made sure he used plenty of lube and eased his way into me to ensure I wouldn't be in any pain.

Other people I have been with before have wanted to do anal, but they never had lube. They wanted to get their dick wet any way they could, which didn't work for me whatsoever.

With Brandon, he likes to cherish my body and make sure that I'm okay no matter what we're doing. He's what I would call a real man though, so it makes sense. The guys my age want to fuck you and keep it moving, but for some reason Brandon always comes back for more.

I take my mind off the rabbit hole I'm going down and focus on what is going to happen when I walk through his doors. I have a spare key to his house, so once I arrive I hop out the car, lock it behind me, and make my way inside the front door.

"Brandon, I'm back," I yell in a sing-song voice.

"I'll be down in a minute," he calls from upstairs.

A minute is always forever with him, so I head to his kitchen and find the bottle of wine we were enjoying last night. I pour both of us a glass of the dry, red wine and admire the deep red color while I wait for Brandon to make an appearance.

## CHAPTER 4

*Brandon*

The conversation with Natalya earlier really has my brain spinning about if she will just walk away from us after everything we have gone through this past year.

When she left this morning, I took some time to reflect on everything and realized that I can't let her go.

Valentine's Day might be in a few days, but there's no reason for me to wait to show her how much she means to me.

I was getting ready to send her a text message asking her to come over, but she beat me to it.

I HEAR NATALYA WALK THROUGH THE FRONT door which causes me to look down at the clock to see what time it is.

Five minutes to 5:00 PM. *Great, I still have some time.*

I decided to decorate the master bedroom with candles and flower petals to make her feel special and seen by me. I've never been the grand gesture kind of guy, so I hope she likes what I have to offer her today.

Once I'm done setting up the room, I head to the bathroom where I freshen up and squirt some cologne on that smells like patchouli. I haven't worn this scent since one of the first times we were together, so I hope this brings us back full circle to when we first were alone together.

*Today I invited Natalya over. Maybe against my better judgement because her and my son did date a little bit ago. It's so weird because we instantly had this spark, that neither of us could let go. There's just something about this girl that lights up a room and makes a guy's heart beat faster than normal.*

*I've been so nervous to see what she thinks about being alone with me, especially after the amicable breakup with my son. I'm sure everything will be just fine.*

*I keep watching the time and noon is finally here. Ding Dong. I can feel my hands start to get clammy with the ring of the doorbell, but I don't know why. My house is clean and* the scent of patchouli lines my skin. There's literally nothing that could go wrong.

I make my way to the front door and there she is. She is so beautiful with her dirty blonde hair, hazel eyes, and flowy blue dress.

"Come on in," I say with a smile while guiding her into the direction of the kitchen.

This isn't her first time being here, so she knows where she is going for the most part. I just don't want to make things awkward by assuming she wants to just freely walk into the house.

When we get to the kitchen she places a bottle of red wine on the counter.

"I brought this red wine for us to enjoy. I haven't tried this one before, but the store representative said it would be a good one if you like dry wines," she says as she continues to look down at the wine bottle.

I make my way over to the drawer that has the wine opener in it and grab two red wine glasses. I look over and see her biting the corner of her lip like she's afraid of what is to happen next.

"You know you don't have to be nervous around me, right?"

I can see a small smile form from the corner of her lips. "I know, it's just different being here with you alone."

I pour both of us a glass of wine and stretch my hand out to her, "maybe a little sip of wine will help calm your nerves."

Luckily, the little sip of wine did make her more

*comfortable. The night continued to go on so well and the conversations were so great, that I didn't want her to leave. So she didn't for the night.*

THINKING BACK ON THAT NIGHT, I KNOW how good Natalya felt. If I can give her a moment similar to then, I will.

I make my way downstairs to the kitchen where I see her facing the counter. Her dirty blonde hair is in curls and she's standing in a black robe.

I sit and admire her for a minute, before slowly creeping my way over to her. Wrapping my arms around her waist from behind, I can smell the perfume that I love so much.

"You smell amazing," I say as my eyes turn to the bottle of wine she has. It's the same one from the very first night we had together. *Fuck, this really is a sign.*

"You don't smell too bad yourself," she says, turning to face me.

I can see her cleavage slowly peaking out of her robe and it's already getting my dick hard. From what I can tell, it's not looking like there is much underneath the robe.

I scoop her up and place her on the counter

where her legs are straddling both sides of me. I know she can see the hunger that fills my eyes. We're supposed to be eating spaghetti for dinner, but I think she's going to be the meal instead.

"Can we talk about earlier," she begins to say before I interrupt her by planting a kiss on her lips.

"How about I see what's underneath this robe instead. Maybe later we can talk. How does that sound?" I ask as I start to plant kisses down her neck.

"Fine," she lets out as she starts to undo her robe.

*Fuck. She looks so sexy with her red lingerie on.*

"Baby girl, you are sexy as hell. I'm so ready to devour every inch of your body."

I can see the sly grin come across her face like she knows what she's doing to me.

I slowly bring the robe down her arms and let it drop onto the counter top. I can't take it completely off because of how she is sitting, but it will work for now.

She's definitely in for it tonight. She doesn't even know what is set up for her upstairs just yet either.

"You should wear these lingerie sets more often. I love the way it shows off your body," I say while pinching the tip of her nipple through her top. I can tell this is starting to turn her on because she lets out a low moan.

"Brandon, you know my nipples are sensitive."

Both of her nipples are pierced which is always fun for me. I can easily torture her in a good way by grabbing onto her nipple piercings or sucking on them.

"Baby girl, you know that's not going to stop me. I love the way your body reacts to me when I touch them."

I reach around the back of her top and unclasp it allowing it to fall to the ground. I take a moment to take in all of her beauty before I bring her right nipple into my mouth, as I cup her left breast.

I slowly nip at her, causing her head to fall back in pleasure.

"Stop teasing me, can you fuck me already?" She asks with need.

I shake my head no as I begin to plant kisses along her stomach, "you're going to have to wait until I get to taste every inch of your body."

Pushing her panties to the side, I plant a teasing kiss onto her.

"Your pussy is already dripping for me, Nat."

Before she can say anything, I plunge my tongue inside of her causing her to gasp from how unexpected it was.

Her hands immediately get tangled in my hair as she moans out in-between licks.

I insert two fingers into her and fuck her with them in a rapid pace, bringing her over the edge with pleasure.

# CHAPTER 5
## Natalya

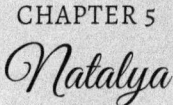

F uck, coming over here I knew what I was getting myself into with the way I'm dressed, but I didn't think he would dive right in.

After he gets me off with his fingers, I think we're finally done with me. I want to make sure he gets the pleasure he deserves too.

"Well fuck Brandon. You've taken your turn, now it's mine."

I get ready to hop off the counter to get on my knees to unbuckle his pants, but he picks me up instead.

"Baby girl, I'm just getting started on you. Tonight is the night that I make everything up to you."

*Make things up to me? Shit, he already made things up to me.*

As he starts to carry me towards the stairs, I try to squirm in his arms causing him to smack my ass.

"I wouldn't try to squirm because I'm not putting you down just yet."

"Fine, but wait until I torture you when we get up these stairs."

He begins to let out a laugh. I hope he knows that I'm serious. He continues to trek up the stairs with me over his shoulder before placing me down inside his bedroom.

I'm in complete awe with what I see around me. He has candles lining the walls with rose petals scattered everywhere. Before I know it, I can feel tears begin falling down my cheeks.

"Nat, don't cry. We're having a good time, so I don't want you to be sad," he says cupping my face.

"These aren't sad tears," I say while punching him in the arm. "They're actually happy tears because this has never happened to me before. I can tell how much thought you put into everything today."

He brings me in for a hug, "let's not get too sappy right now. We're just getting started with the fun."

I'm still in awe with the thought this man has put into everything when he didn't have to. I want to talk about it, but I know I can wait until later to do it.

He instantly pulls me from my thoughts when he grabs my hand to escort me over to the bed.

"You better not get one of these rose petals inside of me," I say with a laugh.

"That should be the least of your worries right now," he says as he pulls my panties down.

"Now, why am I the only naked one here," I continue to laugh, causing him to do the same.

He instantly pulls his shirt over his head, "here, is this better for you?" He asks with a wink.

I bring myself up on my knees on the bed and start to unbuckle his belt. I know he said this time is about me, but he deserves to feel as good as I do.

"Nat, you don't have to do…," he says before I interrupt him with a kiss.

"How about you shush and let me take care of you, too."

I can see on his face that he is trying to hold back any comments he might want to say as I begin to pull down his pants and boxers.

His cock springs free from his pants causing me to lick my lips at the sight in front of me.

I hop off the bed and bring myself down to my knees right in front of him.

"Nat, you don't have to do this."

I slap his cock. "I know I don't have to, but I want to."

He instantly realizes that he isn't the one who is in control anymore.

I begin to flick the tip of his cock with my tongue, causing him to shudder some. Having a Prince Albert piercing and having some length to him, always has his body instantly responding to me.

I bring the tip of his cock into my mouth and begin to take him in and out. I pick up the pace, taking him as deep into my mouth as I can. He's so big but the more I've sucked him off, the deeper I can go. I start to pick up my pace and gently squeeze his balls at the same time.

"Fuck Nat, I'm about to cum," he says as he tries to pull out of my mouth.

Instead, I continue to use his cock to fuck my mouth until beads of cum shoot down my throat.

## CHAPTER 6

## *Brandon*

I absolutely love the way Natalya takes all of me. Something about the way her soft lips wrap around my cock and her touch on my balls, always has me over the edge in no time.

She has had enough fun though, it's time for me to rock her insides.

"Baby girl, I hope you had fun because it's my turn now."

I can see the fear spread across her face because she knows that I'm about to have her screaming out my name in pleasure. I shouldn't be rough since we had sex this morning, but fuck it. Rough is the way she likes it most.

"Lay down on the bed," I say pointing over to the bed.

She does as I say and immediately opens her legs to welcome me in. I decide to torture her a little at first and dive my face into her folds. I suck her clit and begin to finger fuck her nice and deep.

"Fuck Brandon," she yells out as I begin to hit her g-spot. It's her weakness, so anytime I have a chance to go for it, I do.

"You've been such a naughty girl lately, I want you to feel what my fingers have for you before you take my cock."

Her moans begin to get louder as I insert a third finger into her while continuing to suck her clit. I can feel her body start to shake and before I know it, she squirts all over my face.

*Fuck this turns me on so much more. I love the way my girl's body squirts for me.* I begin to lap up all of her liquids as I slowly pull my fingers out of her, sucking my fingers once they are out.

"Can you please fuck me," she begs.

I reach over to the nightstand and grab a condom. Opening the wrapper, I take the condom and sheath myself in one quick motion.

"Get on your knees," I command and she does as I say.

It's time to have a little fun with my girl.

I begin to slide my cock inside of her. *Fuck she feels so good.*

I reach back over to the nightstand and grab the bottle of lube. I squirt some onto my thumb and slowly insert it into her ass, pumping in and out.

"Fuck, that's a lot," she lets out.

I pick up the pace of fucking her from behind while my finger continues to warm up her ass. I pound into her so hard that she moans out my name louder and louder.

When I know her ass is warmed up for me, I pull my cock out and squirt lube on myself and her asshole.

"Alright baby girl, I want you to take a deep breath and release when I start to push myself in. I will go slowly until you are able to take all of me."

"Okay, I'm ready."

She does as I say as I begin to push my cock inside of her tight ass.

"Fuck baby girl, you're so tight but it feels so good," I let out when I push fully into her. I take things slow with her at first to ensure she can take me fully.

To make a distraction, I bring my fingers up to her clit and rub her in circles as I begin to pick up my pace in her ass.

# CHAPTER 7
## *Natalya*

Brandon always thinks that playing with my clit will bring a big enough distraction to what he is doing to me, but he is super wrong. I can feel the way he is stretching my ass, and I love every part of it. His piercing is such an added pleasure.

He begins to pick up his pace, and I can feel all the pleasure running through my body. He moves his fingers from my clit and slowly drags his hands up my body. Stopping to pinch my nipple before heading up to my neck. I can feel his hand grab my neck and begin to put pressure around it.

"Yes Brandon," I moan as he begins to squeeze harder. Breath play has always been a huge kink of mine and often gets me to the edge quickly.

"Your ass is taking my cock so well," he says as he starts to aggressively pound into me, causing my eyes to roll back and my pussy to pulsate with its release. He slowly starts to release his grip from my neck, and I can feel him begin to twitch inside of me as a sign he just came.

He pulls out of me, heads to the bathroom to throw the condom away, and grabs a washcloth to do his usual routine of cleaning me up. Once he's done, he pulls a t-shirt from his closet and throws it over my head while throwing his boxers back on himself.

Once he has his boxers on, he hops into the bed to snuggle up beside me.

"I will never get tired of…," I say before hesitating with my next words. I should just be focused on how he fucked my brains out and not going back to whatever we are, but I just can't help it. I want him even if he doesn't want me back.

I just need to walk away while I can. I pull myself up to the edge of the bed, but before I can get out, he pulls me back.

"Where do you think you're going?" He questions.

"I'm going home just like I did this morning."

I can tell he doesn't like that answer because he instantly gets out of the bed, comes over to my side, and gets down on his knees.

"Nat, you're not going anywhere. We just had the best sex ever, so don't think you're just going to up and leave without allowing me to say what I have to say."

He takes a deep breath before continuing, so I can see that whatever he has to say is important.

"I would be the dumbest man in the world if I let you go. This past year you have made me into a better man, and I'm thankful I've been able to have this time with you. I spoke to Evan and somehow he already knew that you and I were together. I guess we suck at hiding things," he laughs.

I go to interrupt, but he continues. "I want to be able to continue to grow as a man with you and build something with you. I know setting the room up today was a little gesture, but I want to be able to make more gestures for you. If you would allow me to, I want to be your boyfriend. The boyfriend that you spend time with in the real world and not behind closed doors. What do you say, baby girl?"

This isn't where I thought the night was going to go. I'm actually speechless with his confession. I can feel the tears building inside of me, and I know I'm going to erupt any minute now.

## CHAPTER 8
### *Brandon*

W ell, I didn't think this was the way this was going to go. I didn't want her to cry, but I can tell it's too late. The tears begin to run down her face uncontrollably.

Part of me wishes that I waited until Valentine's Day to have this conversation, but I couldn't wait another minute. I can't just let her walk away from me tonight without her knowing how I feel.

After a moment of hesitation, she asks "what changed your mind?"

"You changed my mind. Seeing how much you care showed me that I needed to man up and stop hiding how much I care about you. The world deserves to know about us. So that's exactly what's going to happen from here on out."

I can finally see the tears going away from her eyes and a smile turn up on her face.

"This is what I've wanted for months now and it's finally happening. I'm so thankful for you," she says as she leans in for a kiss. "Also you don't have to get on your knees, you're going to hurt something old man."

Laughter escapes both of us. "An old man won't fuck you like I've done today." I drop my boxers down before saying "let's go for another round."

AFTER ANOTHER ROUND OF FUCKING, WE lay next to each other on the bed just staring at one another.

"I love you Natalya Rose Williams."

"I love you more Brandon James Patterson."

I know things are just going to go up from here with the two of us.

## CHAPTER 9

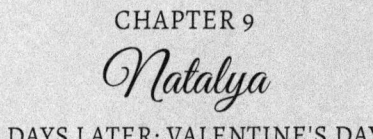

2 DAYS LATER: VALENTINE'S DAY

The past two days with Brandon have gone so well. We have actually went out together in public and didn't get any negative looks like I thought we would. Today, he has some extravagant plan for the two of us to celebrate Valentine's Day, so I'm curious how that's going to go.

He bought me a cute lingerie set that I'm going to slip under my black dress today. I get myself together knowing that he will be here soon to grab me. Instead of wearing my usual perfume, I decide to do something different that smells more like lavender. *I hope he likes the scent.*

I look at myself one more time in the mirror before I hear my doorbell ring. Everything looks like it's in place so I make my way to the door and see him standing in his white collared shirt, black tie, and black pants.

This man is hot as fuck. I still can't believe he belongs to me.

"You're beautiful," he says, planting a kiss on my forehead to not mess up my lipgloss.

"You don't look too bad yourself. What's the plan for tonight?"

He lets out a laugh. "That's for me to know and for you to find out."

Oh, this man has jokes. He knows surprises aren't my thing, but I guess every once in a while I can let him take the lead on things. I grab my bag and make my way to the car where Brandon holds the door open for me.

The car ride to wherever we are going consists of us singing to country music together while he has tried to sneak up my dress. He won't tell me where we're going, so he can't get any early touches.

Before I know it, we are pulling up at a steakhouse that I've been dying to go to for months. There's always a waitlist for the restaurant, so I have no idea how he got us in.

Excitement fills my face. "Babe, you know how much I've wanted to come here. Thank you, thank you, thank you," I say.

"Don't thank me just yet," he says with a grin across his face.

Hmm I have no idea what that means, but I'm just going to go with the flow of things.

When we make our way towards the front door,

the restaurant seems a lot quieter from the outside than I expected it to be for it being 7:00 PM. We make our way inside and I realize there's literally nobody here except the hostess and waitress.

"Right this way Ms. Williams and Mr. Patterson," the hostess says as we make our way back to one of the private booths that's decorated with roses and candles like the bedroom was the other night.

"Did you do this for me?" I ask as a tear rolls down my eye.

"I wanted you to have the best of the best and have a one-on-one experience at your dream restaurant."

I truly have no idea how this man did this, but it has to be the best surprise any man has ever given me before. We sit down and I see a handpicked menu with some of my favorite foods on it on the table.

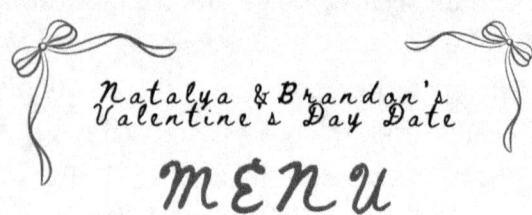

Natalya & Brandon's
Valentine's Day Date

# MENU

## Appetizer

Shrimp cocktail paired with Riesling

## Main Course

Filet Mignon (Medium) with broccoli and
baked potato.
Paired with Cabernet Franc

## Desserts

Chocolate Mousse cake paired with Moscato
Natalya + Brandon

## CHAPTER 10
### *Brandon*

Natalya has been talking about wanting to go to The Steak Cellar for a while now. I'm so happy I knew the owner of the restaurant because he agreed to close his restaurant a few hours earlier, on a holiday at that, to help me make Nat's dreams come true.

I couldn't tell her about tonight because I wanted to see the way her face lit up when we got into the restaurant and she saw that we were the only ones here. I had a special menu curated for the two of us with all of her favorite foods that she's talked about over the past year.

As she looks it over she begins to tear up. "You really do pay attention to me," she says as the waitress brings over the wine and the appetizer.

"Of course I do, baby girl. I want to make sure you have everything you like and make you feel special. It's crazy how much we have gone through this year together, but I wouldn't choose for things to go any other way. You bring happiness to me everyday, and I don't want anyone else in this world."

We take some bites of the appetizer in-between our conversation.

"I wouldn't be where I am right now if I didn't have you by my side. There were so many days that I struggled, but knowing I have you to be with at the end of the day keeps me going."

I take her hands in mine and stare into her eyes for a little bit just thinking about how far we truly have come.

Before I can say what else is on my mind, the chef comes out with the main course.

"Hey Brandon and Natalya. I have prepared this filet mignon with a baked potato and broccoli for you all as your main course. I hope you both enjoy," he says as he places our meals in front of us. Behind him comes our waitress with our next wine that pairs with the steak.

"This is amazing, babe. You did wonderful."

"I only want what's best for my girl."

She takes a bite of her steak, and she is in absolute awe. "This tastes delicious," she exclaims.

"The chef definitely knows how to make a great meal, I'm so glad you like it."

We continue making small talk as we eat, but I

hope she is ready for what I have to ask her when the dessert comes out.

The waitress comes over and brings out our last wine followed by our dessert. "I hope you all enjoy your chocolate mousse cake paired with moscato."

She immediately takes a bite of the cake. "Oh my gosh, this cake is to die for."

"I'm glad you're enjoying it. I do have something I want to ask you," I say, while taking a box out of my pocket.

Her face fills with confusion when she eyes the box.

"Natalya, you really have been a joy to my life over the past few years. I know in the next few months your lease will be up on your apartment, so I would love it if you would move in with me," I say while opening the box to a house key.

She lets out a laugh. "You know I already have a house key, right?"

*Fuck, that is right.*

"Just ignore that part. You wanna move in?" I say with a laugh.

"Hell yeah, let's go home and have round two of dessert."

She instantly stands up and grabs her belongings so we can make our way back to our home. We barely make it through the front door before we start ripping each other's clothes off.

"I see you're wearing that matching set I bought you."

"Shush it and just fuck me already," she says as she pushes me over to the couch.

Oh hell no, she's not about to be in control tonight.

"Bend your ass over this couch," I say while grabbing my tie to bind her hands together. I smack her ass a few times before rubbing my fingers against her slick folds. "I see you're already wet for me."

"Maybe just a little," she looks back to say with a face of need.

Shoot, that was my sign right there to destroy her pussy.

"I need to go grab a condom," I say while pulling away.

"Just fuck me, it'll be okay."

I do as she says. I fuck her so hard to the point she's not going to be able to walk tomorrow. Once we're done, I unbind her hands.

"Happy Valentine's Day babe," I say as I plant a kiss on her forehead.

# Acknowledgments

To my elite team (Emma, Hilary, and Erica), thank you for reading the books I throw at you and helping me spruce them up for others to get.

To my alpha/beta readers (Alicia, Carisa, Stephanie, Jami, Lillith, Sandy, and Liane), thank you for providing feedback on the book to get it ready for readers to get it in their hands.

To my street team, thank you for helping me promote this book and all of my other books!

To my readers, thank you so much for picking up my books and supporting me while I go on this rollercoaster of a journey as an author.

# *About the Author*

Deann Soleil is a self-published author based in Virginia who focuses on writing forbidden romances. When not writing, she is a full-time social worker who works with victims of community violence to help them overcome their traumatic experiences. If you're looking for short, fast-paced books, then look no further.

# Also by Deann Soleil

Consumed by the Professor

Chasing the Forbidden Desire

Stalked Through the Night

A Twisted Thanksgiving Holiday

Best Christmas Ever

**Anthologies:**

A Wild Run Anthology (The Chase)

Monsters, Masks & Mayhem Anthology (The Graveyard)

A Merry Little Romance (The Best Friend Holiday Cabin Trip)

Just A Taste - Richmond: A SaSS Anthology (Signed with Love)

Christmas Temptation Anthology (One Stop at Love)